W9-BCS-933

What if...?

For a free color catalog describing Gareth Stevens' list of high-quality books, call 1-800-341-3569 (USA) or 1-800-461-9120 (Canada).

ISBN 0-8368-1090-2

This edition first published in 1994 by
Gareth Stevens Publishing
1555 North RiverCenter Drive, Suite 201
Milwaukee, Wisconsin 53212, USA

Original edition first published in Great Britain in 1993 by ABC, All Books for Children, a division of The All Children's Company Ltd., London. Text and illustrations © 1993 by Peter Utton.

Printed in the United States of America
1 2 3 4 5 6 7 8 9 99 98 97 96 95 94

At this time, Gareth Stevens, Inc., does not use 100 percent recycled paper, although the paper used in our books does contain about 30 percent recycled fiber. This decision was made after a careful study of current recycling procedures revealed their dubious environmental benefits. We will continue to explore recycling options.

Title 11 094-C2-96

What if...?

Written and illustrated
by Peter Utton

Gareth Stevens Publishing
MILWAUKEE

What if... just as the wounded soldier climbs up the last jagged bit of mountain, he sees, through the mists of time, the door to a warm and cozy cave?

But **what if…**

just as he reaches the door to the
warm and cozy cave, he sees . . .

a hideous, smelly monster
from outer space
who has gotten
there first
and is about
to drink
his milk?

And **what if...**, just at that moment, a space-cleaning machine comes and sucks up the monster and rushes it off to a hideous, smelly planet where it can be hideous, smelly, and happy?

Phew! That was close! But **what if...**

someone has left open the door
to the secret tunnel . . .

and the secret tunnel
has been discovered
by a band of
bloodthirsty
pirates searching
for treasure?

Phew! That was close! But **what if**...

that isn't really his baby sister
asleep in her crib . . .

but a giant-hairy-
octopus-spider
waiting to
ambush
innocent
travelers?

21

But
what if...

22

just in the nick of time, a giant-hairy-octopus-spider-eating bird (who's on our side) swoops down and drags the giant-hairy-octopus-spider off for its supper?

Phew! That was close!

But **what if...** the bedroom door
should suddenly start to open . . .

but it's only Pegasus, his trusty
wonder horse,

who's come to rescue his lord
and master?

Phew! That was close!